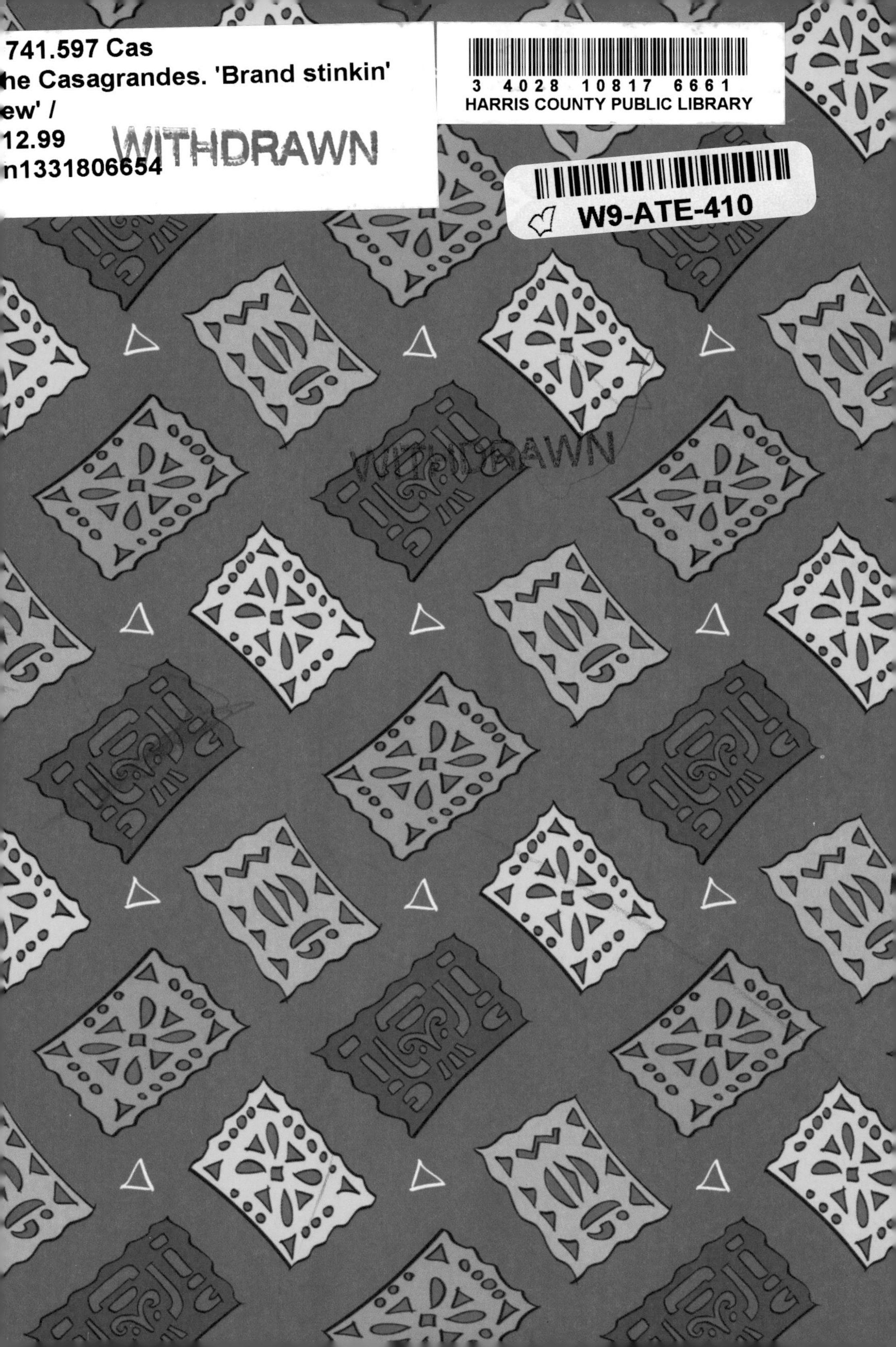

THE CASAGRANDES
"BRAND STINKIN' NEW"
PAPERCUTZ
New York

#3 "BRAND STINKIN' NEW"

"CUT AND RUN"
Derek Fridolfs — Writer
Amanda Tran — Artist, Colorist
Wilson Ramos Jr. — Letterer

"CHEER UP"
Paloma Uribe — Writer
Kelsey Wooley — Artist, Colorist
Wilson Ramos Jr. — Letterer

"LALO FOREVER"
Paloma Uribe — Writer
Zazo Aguiar — Artist, Colorist
Wilson Ramos Jr. — Letterer

"OLD SOLE"
Amanda Fein — Writer
Zazo Aguiar — Artist, Colorist
Wilson Ramos Jr. — Letterer

"SICKBED RIVALRY"
Kacey Huang-Wooley — Writer
D.K. Terrell — Artist, Colorist
Wilson Ramos Jr. — Letterer

"PRANKS FOR NOTHING"
Derek Fridolfs — Writer
Lex Hobson— Artist, Colorist
Wilson Ramos Jr. — Letterer

"FUSION FOR A BRUISIN'"
Caitlyn Connelly — Writer
Jennifer Hernandez — Artist, Colorist
Wilson Ramos Jr. — Letterer

"CASA TO THE MOON"
Paloma Uribe — Writer
Zazo Aguiar — Artist, Colorist
Wilson Ramos Jr. — Letterer

"LEAVE A MESSAGE AT THE BAWK!"
Amanda Fein — Writer
Zazo Aguiar — Artist, Colorist
Wilson Ramos Jr. — Letterer

"A SUPER HARRRD CHOICE"
Derek Fridolfs — Writer
Izzy Boyce Blanchard — Artist
Erin Rodriguez — Colorist
Wilson Ramos Jr. — Letterer

"LATE AGAIN"
Paloma Uribe — Writer
Zazo Aguiar — Artist, Colorist
Wilson Ramos Jr. — Letterer

"A TIE GAME"
Derek Fridolfs — Writer
Daniela Rodriguez — Artist, Colorist
Wilson Ramos Jr. — Letterer

"TRASH OR TREASURE"
Caitlyn Connelly — Writer
Lex Hobson — Artist, Colorist
Wilson Ramos Jr. — Letterer

"SERGIO'S BIG BREAK"
Paloma Uribe — Writer
Zazo Aguiar — Artist, Colorist
Wilson Ramos Jr. — Letterer

"A BLANKET STATEMENT"
Derek Fridolfs — Writer
Amanda Tran — Artist, Colorist
Wilson Ramos Jr. — Letterer

"LIMITED EDITION"
Jair Holguin — Writer
Amanda Lioi — Artist
Lex Hobson — Colorist
Wilson Ramos Jr. — Letterer

AMANDA TRAN — Cover Artist
Preview "SLEEPLESS IN PRESCHOOL" Kara Fein — Writer; Amanda Lioi — Artist, Colorist; Wilson Ramos Jr. — Letterer
JAMES SALERNO — Sr. Art Director/Nickelodeon
JAYJAY JACKSON — Design
KRISTEN G. SMITH, DANA CLUVERIUS, MOLLIE FREILICH, NEIL WADE, MIGUEL PUGA, LALO ALCARAZ,
JOAN HILTY, KRISTEN YU-UM, EMILIE CRUZ, and ARTHUR "DJ" DESIN — Special Thanks
KARLO ANTUNES — Editor
STEPHANIE BROOKS — Assistant Managing Editor
JEFF WHITMAN— Comics Editor/Nickelodeon
MICOL HIATT — Comics Designer/Nickelodeon
JIM SALICRUP
Editor-in-Chief

ISBN: 978-1-5458-0911-2 paperback edition
ISBN: 978-1-5458-0910-5 hardcover edition

www.papercutz.com

Papercutz books may be purchased for business or promotional use. For information on bulk purchases please contact Macmillan Corporate and Premium Sales Department at (800) 221-7945 x5442.

Printed in India
May 2022

Distributed by Macmillan
First Printing

THE CASAGRANDES

Theme Song Performed by: ALLY BROOKE
Theme Song Composed by: GERMAINE FRANCO
Lyrics by: GERMAINE FRANCO, MIKE RUBINER & LALO ALCARAZ
Rap Lyrics Performed by: IZABELLA ALVAREZ

I'm in the big city with my big familia [family]

Everyday here is my favorite día [day]

One big house and our family store
Food and laughter ¡y mucho amor! [and a lot of love!]

Tíos [aunts and uncles], abuelos [grandparents], all of my primos [cousins]...

A dog, a parrot, amigos! [friends!]

We're one big family now!
Sundays and Mondays
They're all fun days when you're with the...
Casagrandes!
¡Mucha vida! [A lot of life!]

Casagrandes!
¡Bienvenida! [Welcome!]

Casagrandes!
¡Mucha risa! [A lot of laughs!]

Casagrandes!
We're all familia! [Family!]

¡Tan-tan! [Tah-dah!]

MEET THE CASAGRANDES *and friends!*

RONNIE ANNE SANTIAGO

Ronnie Anne's a skateboarding city girl now. She's fearless, free-spirited, and always quick to come up with a plan. She's one tough cookie, but she also has a sweet side. Ronnie Anne loves helping her family, and that's taught her to help others too. When she's not pitching in at the family *mercado*, you can find her exploring the neighborhood with her best friend Sid, or ordering hot dogs with her skater buds Casey, Nikki, and Sameer. Having a family as big as the Casagrandes has taught Ronnie Anne to deal with anything life throws her way.

BOBBY SANTIAGO

Bobby is Ronnie Anne's big bro. He's a student and one of the hardest workers in the city. He loves his family and loves working at the *mercado*. As his *abuelo's* right hand man, Bobby can't wait to take over the family business one day. He's a big kid at heart, and his clumsiness gets him into some sticky situations at work, like locking himself in the freezer. Mercado mishaps aside, everyone in the neighborhood loves to come to the store and talk to Bobby.

MARIA CASAGRANDE SANTIAGO

Maria is Bobby and Ronnie Anne's mom. As a nurse at the city hospital, she's hardworking and even harder to gross out. For years, Maria, Bobby, and Ronnie Anne were used to only having each other… but now that they've moved in with their Casagrande relatives, they're embracing big family life. Maria is the voice of reason in the household and known for her always-on-the-go attitude. Her long work hours means she doesn't always get to spend time with Bobby and Ronnie Anne; but when she does, she makes that time count.

HECTOR CASAGRANDE

Hector is Carlos and Maria's dad, and the *abuelo* of the family (that means grandpa)! He owns the *mercado* on the ground floor of their apartment building and takes great pride in his work, his family, and being the unofficial "mayor" of the block. He loves to tell stories, share his ideas, and gossip (even though he won't admit to it). You can find him working in the *mercado*, playing guitar, or watching his favorite *telenovela*.

ROSA CASAGRANDE

Rosa is Carlos and Maria's mom and the *abuela* of the family (that means grandma)! She's the head of the household, the wisest Casagrande, and the master cook with a superhuman ability to tell when anyone in the house is hungry. She often tries to fix problems or illnesses with traditional Mexican home remedies and potions. She's very protective of her family… sometimes a little too much.

CARLOS CASAGRANDE

Carlos is Maria's brother. He's married to Frida, and together they have four kids: Carlota, C.J., Carl, and Carlitos. Carlos is a Professor of Cultural Studies at a local college. Usually he has his head in the clouds or his nose in a textbook. Relatively easygoing, Carlos is a loving father and an enthusiastic teacher who tries to get his kids interested in their Mexican heritage.

FRIDA PUGA CASAGRANDE

Frida is Carlota, C.J., Carl, and Carlitos' mom. She's an art professor and a performance artist, and is always looking for new ways to express herself. She's got a big heart and isn't shy about her emotions. Frida tends to cry when she's sad, happy, angry, or any other emotion you can think of. She's always up for fun, is passionate about her art, and loves her family more than anything.

CARLOTA CASAGRANDE

Carlota is CJ, Carl, and Carlitos' older sister. A social media influencer, she's excited to be like a big sister to Ronnie Anne. She's a force to be reckoned with, and is always trying to share her distinctive vintage style tips with Ronnie Anne.

CJ (CARLOS JR.) CASAGRANDE

CJ is Carlota's younger brother and Carl and Carlitos' older brother. He was born with Down Syndrome. He lights up any room with his infectious smile and is always ready to play. He's obsessed with pirates and is BFFs with Bobby. He likes to wear a bowtie to any family occasion, and you can always catch him laughing or helping his *abuela*.

CARL CASAGRANDE

Carl is wise beyond his years. He's confident, outgoing, and puts a lot of time and effort into looking good. He likes to think of himself as a suave businessman and doesn't like to get caught playing with his action figures or wearing his footie PJs. Even though Bobby is nothing but nice to him, Carl sees his big cousin as his biggest rival.

CARLITOS CASAGRANDE

Carlitos is the baby of the family, and is always copying the behavior of everyone in the household—even if they aren't human. He's a playful and silly baby who loves to play with the family pets.

LALO

Lalo is a slobbery bull mastiff who thinks he's a lapdog. He's not the smartest pup, and gets scared easily… but he loves his family and loves to cuddle.

SERGIO

Sergio is the Casagrandes' beloved pet parrot. He's a blunt, sassy bird who "thinks" he's full of wisdom and always has something to say. The Casagrandes have to keep a close eye on their credit card as Sergio is addicted to online shopping and is always asking the family to buy him some new gadget he saw on TV. Sergio is most loyal to Rosa and serves as her wing-man, partner-in-crime, taste-tester, and confidant. Sergio is quite popular in the neighborhood and is always up for a good time. When he's not working part time at the *mercado* (aka messing with Bobby), he can be found hanging with his roommate Ronnie Anne, partying with Sancho and his other pigeon pals, or trying to get his ex-girlfriend, Priscilla (an ostrich at the zoo), to respond to him.

SID CHANG

Sid is Ronnie Anne's quirky best friend. She's new to the city but dives headfirst into everything she finds interesting. She and her family just moved into the apartment one floor above the Casagrandes. In fact, Sid's bedroom is right above Ronnie Anne's. A dream come true for any BFFs.

CASEY

Casey is a happy-go-lucky kid who's always there to help. He knows all the best spots to get grub in Great Lakes City. When he is not skateboarding with the crew, he loves working with his dad, Alberto, on their Cubano sandwich food truck.

SAMEER

Sameer is a goofy sweetheart who wishes he was taller, but what he lacks in height, he makes up for with his impressive hair and sweet skate moves. He is always down for the unexpected adventure and loves entertaining his friends with his spooky tales!

NIKKI

Nikki is as daring as she is easygoing and laughs when she is nervous. When she's not hanging with her buds at the skatepark, she likes checking out the newest sneakers and reading books about the paranormal.

LAIRD

Laird is a total team player and the newest member of Ronnie Anne's friends. Despite often being on the wrong end of misfortune, Laird is an awesome skateboarder who can do tons of tricks…unfortunately stopping is not one of them.

BECKY

A tough as nails classmate of Ronnie Anne and the skater kids. She makes a good match for her girlfriend, Dodge, captain of the Chavez Academy dodgeball team. Becky has a taste for chaos and destruction that she shares with her younger brother, Ricky, and her loyal dog, Malo. In a pinch though, Becky will definitely come through for a friend in need!

LINCOLN LOUD

Lincoln is Ronnie Anne's dearest friend from Royal Woods. They still keep in touch and visit one another as often as they can. He has learned that surviving the Loud household with ten sisters means staying a step ahead. He's the man with a plan, always coming up with a way to get what he wants or deal with a problem, even if things inevitably go wrong. Lincoln's sisters may drive him crazy, but he loves them and is always willing to help out if they need him.

STANLEY CHANG

Stanley Chang is Sid's dad. He's a conductor on the GLART-train that runs through the city. He's a patient man who likes to do Tai Chi when he gets stressed out. He likes to cheer up train commuters with fun facts, but emotionally he breaks down more than the train does.

ADELAIDE CHANG

Adelaide Chang is Sid's little sister. She's 6 years old, and has a flair for the dramatic. You can always find her trying to make her way into her big sister Sid's adventures.

VITO FILLIPONIO

Vito is one of Rosa and Hector's oldest and dearest friends, and a frequent customer at the Mercado. He's lovable, nosy, and usually overstays his welcome, but there is nothing he wouldn't do for his loved ones and his dogs, Big Tony and Little Sal.

BIG TONY & LITTLE SAL

MS GALIANO

Ms. Galiano is Ronnie Anne and the skater kid's teacher at Cesar Chavez Academy. She is sweet as pie and often relies on the kids to keep her up to date on the new, hip, pop culture trends. She briefly dated Ronnie Anne's dad, Arturo, and even though it didn't work out, they still remain friends.

"CUT AND RUN"

THE RIGHT BALANCE OF SPRAY, CONDITIONER, AND GEL.
FOLLOWED BY ONE LAST BRUSH. AND...
PERFECTO!
OKAY. WHAT DO YOU WANT, CJ?
PLAY SUPERHEROES WITH ME!
BUT I SPENT ALL THIS TIME LOOKING GOOD. AND NOW YOU WANT TO MESS THAT UP?
I DON'T WANT TO LOOK SILLY.
NO. SUPERHEROES ALWAYS LOOK SUPER COOL.
I PROMISE!

SUPER CJ!
AND HIS SIDEKICK... SIDEKICK...
¿QUÉ PASÓ?
AHEM.
HIS SIDEKICK CAPITÁN CHOO CHOO.
FLASH
MY HEROES! YOU'VE SAVED THE DAY!
AND I'VE SAVED THIS EVENT WITH MY CAMERA!
BAH. A HERO NEVER REVEALS HIS SECRET IDENTITY!
NICE CHOO-CHOO CHONIES, LITTLE MAN!
END

"LALO FOREVER"

POP
COME ON, GUYS, LET'S HEAD OUT FOR SOME FUN!
FIRST STOP, BRUNO'S HOT DOG CART!
HERE, LALO, YOUR FAVORITE HOT DOG, THE LALO SPECIAL MADE FROM PET-SAFE INGREDIENTS...
HOT DAWG
BARK
BARK
CHOMP
GULP
WHOA, THAT'S RECORD FAST HOT DOG EATING, BUTTERCUP!
BETTER MAKE THAT ANOTHER FULL ONE!

A LITTLE RAIN WON'T STOP US! OH, SORRY, LALO, YOU DON'T QUITE FIT UNDER THE UMBRELLA, YOU DON'T MIND, RIGHT?
OH, LOOK! BUTTERCUP HAS LITTLE RAIN BOOTIES!
AWW, THOSE ARE SO CUTE! BUTTERCUP, YOU'RE THE CUTEST DOG **EVER!**
HMMPH!
NOW THE SUN'S OUT! LET'S FIND A NICE, SHADY SPOT.

BUMMER! OUR SPOT'S TAKEN! SHALL WE GET IT BACK FROM **BIG TONY** AND **LITTLE SAL?**
ZZZZ
YOU'RE NOT VERY INTIMIDATING, LALO...
SNICKER!
GRRR!
WHIMPER!
GOOD TRY, BOY!
GROWL!
HMMN?

BARK
BARK
YELP
YEP
NICE WORK, BUTTERCUP!
SIGH!
YOU'RE STILL MY CUDDLY BIG BEAR, LALO!
MMMM!
BURP!
OH, THAT'S WHERE MY LOLLIPOP WENT TOO, HUH?
SPLAT
END

"SICKBED RIVALRY"

THAT DARN BIRD! I'LL SHOW ROSA WHO SHE CAN REALLY COUNT ON!
THERE! LUNCH FOR THE *FAMILIA* IS DONE!
¡ALMUERZO! WHO WANTS NACHO SOUP?
SORRY, *ABUELO*, SERGIO ALREADY MADE THIS KILLER FRUIT SALAD!
IT'S DELICIOUS **AND** NUTRITIOUS!
POP
FINE! IF I CAN'T COOK, THEN I'LL JUST TAKE CARE OF THE--
CLEANING?

¿PERDÓN? CAN SOMEONE PLEASE BRING ME A GLASS OF WATER?
GOT IT!
I'M COMING!
NO YOU DON'T!
HEY!
SPLASH
SWOOSH
AY! MY BACK!
CRACK
I'M SO GLAD YOU CAN JOIN ME IN BED. I WAS GETTING SO BORED BY MYSELF!
OH, SERGIO? I THINK I NEED ANOTHER PILLOW FOR MY POOR BACK!
I DID **NOT** SIGN UP FOR THIS...
END

"FUSION FOR A BRUISIN"

TURN UP THE HEAT, *ABUELA!*
¡NIÑAS! YOU'RE CROWDING THE PAN... AND ME!
WE NEED THIS PLATED IN FIVE!
YES, CHEF!
YOU GIRLS HAVE BEEN WATCHING TOO MANY COOKING SHOWS!
VOILA! OUR FIRST MEXICAN-CHINESE FUSION DISH: CHORIZO BAO!
WHOA...
¡ÑAM! THIS IS AMAZING!
MORE LIKE ***LIFE-CHANGING!***
WE CAN DO EVEN BETTER! BACK TO THE KITCHEN!
I'LL BE SEEING ***YOU*** LATER.

THOSE ONIONS LOOK MORE DICED THAN MINCED!
SNIFF!
SIZZLE
DAB, FOLD, SQUEEZE!
TAH-DAH! TACO WONTONS, DIM SUM TAMALES, BARBACOA LO MEIN!

¡AY, DIOS MÍO! I'M TIRED, GIRLS!
ALRIGHT, ABUELA, WE'LL TAKE OVER!
WHY SHOULD WE STOP AT MEXICAN-CHINESE FUSION?
WE COULD COMBINE ANYTHING!
EGGS GRADE A
WE ARE CULINARY GENIUSES!
OKAY, MAYBE NOT GENIUSES...

THEY'RE... UH, CREATIVE?
GIRLS!
YOU'VE USED UP ALL OUR GROCERIES FOR THE WEEK!
WELL, AT LEAST WE HAVE THE MEAL PREP DONE.
ABUELA, DID WE DO SOMETHING WRONG? WHY ARE WE BEING *PUNISHED?*
I DON'T KNOW ABOUT YOU GUYS, BUT I LOVE THIS TORTILLA SOUP POP!
SLURP
END

"LEAVE A MESSAGE AT THE BAWK!"

UM, THIS IS THE *MERCADO.* UH, WE'RENOTHERE... BYE!
⇉SQUAWK!⇇ MAYBE WE SHOULD WRITE A SCRIPT?
I'M NOT HERE, I'M SO SORRY, CUSTOMER! I SHOULD HAVE BEEN HERE WHEN YOU NEEDED ME!
MAYBE ***SIXTY-THIRD*** TIME'S THE CHARM?
⇉SIGH,⇇ MAYBE WE SHOULD GIVE UP, ***SERGIO***. WE'VE BEEN AT THIS FOR HOURS.
DON'T WORRY, BOBBY...
⇉BRAWK!⇇ JUST FOLLOW MY LEAD.
¡HOLA! YOU HAVE REACHED THE *MERCADO.* SORRY, WE'RE NOT IN RIGHT NOW...
WE WILL RETURN YOUR CALL SHORTLY. PLEASE LEAVE A MESSAGE AT THE--
HOLA, ROBERTO! HOW'S THE VOICE MESSAGE?
IT WAS... ALMOST PERFECT. ⇉SIGH.⇇
END

"LATE AGAIN"

UGH. ABUELA'S PLAYING CUMBIA ALREADY? WHAT TIME IS IT?
CROSSING
HOT DOGG
-GASP!- I'M LATE FOR SCHOOL! WHERE'S MY HOODIE?
¡ADIÓS, ABUELA! SEE YOU LATER!
ADIÓS, BE CAREFUL!
WHOA...
I DIDN'T KNOW TÍA FRIDA'S WORKING ON ANOTHER ART PROJECT!

GOOD THING LAIRD'S BEEN TEACHING ME SOME YOGA MOVES, HERE WE GO!
EXHALE, WARRIOR TWO! ALMOST THERE.
MMM! FRESH AIR! ALRIGHT NOTHING'S STOPPING ME NOW!
DANG IT, I STEPPED ON DOG POO?! UGH! I'LL GO CHANGE MY SHOES.
SQUISH
ONE FOOT YOGA, WHY NOT? HAHA! I'M GONNA BE BETTER THAN LAIRD SOON!
SOON...
ALRIGHT, READY TO--WHAT!?

UGH! WHY DOES THERE HAVE TO BE A 5K CAT RUN TODAY?
MEOW
MEOW
STOMP
YES, I MADE IT! ...WAIT, WHAT'S EVERYONE DOING OUTSIDE?
Z ACADEMY
... SO AFTER MY MORNING YOGA ROUTINE, I TAKE A WALK WITH MY THERAPY TORTOISE, MOZART! IT MAKES ME FEEL CALM AND READY TO TAKE ON THE DAY! THANKS FOR LETTING ME BRING HIM, MS. GALIANO.
OOO!
THANK YOU FOR SHARING YOUR MORNING ROUTINE WITH US, LAIRD! RONNIE ANNE, YOU'RE JUST IN TIME, IT'S YOUR TURN!
I DECIDED IT'D BE FUN TO SOAK IN THE MORNING SUN WHILE WE TALK ABOUT OUR MORNING ROUTINES!
FUNNY THING, MY MORNING ROUTINE INVOLVES SOME YOGA TOO...
END

"TRASH OR TREASURE"

CARLOTA, I THINK IT'S TIME TO DONATE SOME OF THESE CLOTHES...
FINE, BUT YOU HAVE TO GO THROUGH YOUR STUFF TOO!
WHAT STUFF?
THIS STUFF!
SENTIMENTAL T-SHIRTS
JUNK
MY SHIRT! I WAS WEARING THAT SHIRT WHEN CARL USED THE BIG-BOY POTTY FOR THE FIRST TIME!
WELL, MOST OF IT MADE IT TO THE POTTY...
NOW LET'S START THIS PURGE!

DONATE, DONATE, DONATE!
OH, I REMEMBER THIS BEAR...
IT WAS ON MY FIRST DATE WITH YOUR FATHER...
YOU'RE MY HONEY
...THAT I SPOTTED IT IN THE GUTTER!
YOU'RE MY HONEY
MOM, MAYBE NOT SO CLOSE TO YOUR FACE...

CARLOTA, PLEASE JUST LET ME KEEP IT!
IT'S A USED TISSUE, MOM!
BUT IT'S FROM YOUR FIRST DANCE RECITAL!
I CRIED SO MUCH SEEING MY *MIJA* UP ON THE STAGE. ⇉SNIFF!⇇ SEE? IT STILL WORKS!

I'M REALLY PROUD OF YOU, MOM.
THANK YOU, SWEETIE. YOU KNOW IT'S HARD FOR ME TO LET GO...
MOM!
WELL, WE DID IT!
I CAN'T BELIEVE THEY DIDN'T WANT MY TISSUE... IT'S VINTAGE!
I HAVE SOMETHING THAT WILL CHEER YOU UP. *ABUELA!*

I DON'T KNOW WHAT COULD POSSIBLY REPLACE --
WHAT IS THAT?
CARLOTA ASKED ME TO FIND A WAY TO SAVE THESE OLD T-SHIRTS, SO I MADE YOU A QUILT!
YOU'RE MY HONEY
Mother & Son CAMP TRIP
World's Best Mom
¡MAMI! CARLOTA! THIS IS THE GREATEST GIFT EVER!
NOW I CAN FINALLY WEAR ALL MY MEMORIES AT ONCE!
STILL GOT THAT TISSUE?
END

"A BLANKET STATEMENT"

THERE!
I SEE IT TOO!
HOW CAN YOU NOT SEE IT? HE HAS IT IN EVERY PHOTO!
¡JA!
¡JA!
¡JA!
¡JA!
¡JA!
¡JA!
HRRRK
RMMMM
FINE, LAUGH IT UP. BUT MARK MY WORDS...
I'LL NEVER BE SEEN WITH MY--I MEAN A BLANKIE EVER AGAIN!
FOOTIE PJS AND A BLANKIE. GREAT COMBO!
HAHAHA!

CARL? SWEETIE?
IT'S NOTHING TO BE ASHAMED OF. COME BACK AND JOIN US.

OH, DEAR.
DON'T WORRY. I'LL KEEP YOUR SECRET. THE OTHERS DON'T HAVE TO KNOW.
THIS IS JUST BETWEEN YOU AND ME.
FLASH
END

"CHEER UP"

UGH! SO TIRED!
AAAHH!
SIP
SIP
DING DING
CHOMP
CRUNCH
CRUNCH
HOW ARE YOU DOING, RONNIE ANNE?
I HAD 5 TESTS TODAY! IT'S LIKE TEACHERS PLAN THIS ON PURPOSE OR SOMETHING, I HOPE I DID ALRIGHT.
DON'T WORRY, YOU GOT THIS!

MY TAKE HOME TEST DIDN'T EVEN MAKE IT TO SCHOOL TODAY!
A BUNNY SNUCK INTO MY ROOM AND ATE IT!
GNAW
CHOMP
CHOMP
GNAW
YOU PROBABLY ACED EVERYTHING, RONNIE ANNE! UNLIKE MY WRETCHED DATE LAST NIGHT!
LADIES AND GENTLEMEN, SIT BACK AND ENJOY THE MOVIE!
WANT A TURKEY LEG?
SHHH!
GASP!

RONALDA, YOU'RE HOME! THE FIDEO IS ABOUT TO COME OUT, YOUR FAVORITE!
YOU'LL BE AS HAPPY AS THIS TORTILLA!
SPLOOSH
SORRY, THAT MADE ME LAUGH.
IT'S READY!
HEY!
¡GRACIAS, ABUELA Y ABUELO! YOU'VE MADE MY DAY!
DE NADA, RONNIE ANNE.
END

"OLD SOLE"

SIGH! RO, I NEED TO RECORD ANOTHER VIDEO TODAY FOR MY ME-TUBE CHANNEL, BUT I'M OUT OF IDEAS!
I'M SORRY, CARLOTA. LET'S HOPE LOOKING THROUGH YOUR OLD CONTENT HELPS.
"OLD"... THAT'S IT! I SHOULD MAKE A VINTAGE FASHION VIDEO! RONNIE ANNE, CANCEL OUR PLANS. IT'S TIME TO GO THRIFTING!
GOOD THING I BROUGHT A SNACK...
...I HAD A FEELING WE WEREN'T GOING TO LUNCH TODAY.
WOW, THIS DRESS IS GRUNGY AND CUTE!
AND STAIN-FREE! WHAT A FIND!
LOOKIN' GOOD.
THIS JACKET IS PERF! NOW, FOR SHOES...
OXFORD HEELS? ARMY BOOTS? HOW DOES THIS STORE NOT SELL SHOES?!
YAWN! WE DON'T SELL THEM. PROBABLY, BECAUSE THEY DIDN'T WEAR SHOES BACK IN THE DAY.
THAT DOESN'T SOUND RIGHT...

SIGH! NOTHING WORKS!
I'M SORRY WE COULDN'T FIND THE RIGHT SHOES FOR YOUR VIDEO. WE CAN ALWAYS TRY AGAIN TOMORROW.
BUT I WANTED TO SHOOT TODAY! I GUESS I CAN JUST SHOW MY OUTFIT FROM THE KNEES UP...
import Gifts
OR NOT! MOM, THOSE ARE THE CUTEST PLATFORM SANDALS I'VE EVER SEEN!
THESE OL' THINGS? THANKS, MIJA!
HI, GUYS! TODAY, I'M GOING TO SHOW YOU...
...HOW TO CREATE THE PERFECT VINTAGE OUTFIT...
...WITH THE PERFECT VINTAGE SHOES.
IT'S SO COOL YOU KEPT THOSE SANDALS FROM WAY BACK WHEN, TIA FRIDA.
OH, THOSE AREN'T VINTAGE. I BOUGHT THEM RECENTLY.
IT'S SO GREAT WHEN OLD TRENDS COME BACK!
END

"PRANKS FOR NOTHING"

Brain
Spine
Teeth
Gills
Heart
Stomach
THE GREAT WHITE SHARK HAS A TREMENDOUS BRAIN IN ADDITION TO BEING AN EFFICIENT HUNTER.
TO BE MORE CLEVER THAN ITS PREY, IT HAS TO HAVE ENOUGH BRAINS TO OUTSMART THEM.
!
SHE'S LIKE A SHARK STALKING ME IN OPEN WATER!
RING
RING
SAY, UNCLE, I'LL SEE YOU AT HOME.
RONNIE ANNE?!
WHAT'S WRONG? LOST YOUR APPETITE?
RUMBLE

HAVE A NICE DAY, TIO!
GOT TO GET TO SCHOOL BEFORE SOMETHING HAPPENS.
TAP-TAP-TAP-TAP
TAP-TAP-TAP-TAP
ALMOST HOME... YEAH.... ALMOST HOME.
CLINK
CLANK

OH, IT'S YOU.
RONNIE ANNE! I CAN'T TAKE IT ANYMORE! PLEASE, JUST GET IT OVER WITH!
WHAT WAS YOUR PRANK?!
THE PRANK?
OOOOH... THERE WAS NO PRANK. I GUESS THAT'S KIND OF A PRANK IN ITSELF.
IS THAT WHY YOU'RE LATE?
YOU TOTALLY MISSED THE SHARK WEEK PARTY WE THREW FOR YOU.
SORRY YOU MISSED IT. BUT THERE'S ALWAYS NEXT YEAR.
SIGH!
END

"CASA TO THE MOON!"

BEAUTIFUL *FLORES* FOR A BEAUTIFUL *DÍA*!
GRAB THEM !
BLAST OFF!
WOO-HOO!
PFFFFT
ZOOM
BUT HOW ARE WE HERE? THIS IS NOT POSSIBLE!
¡CLARO QUE SÍ!, WE'RE ON THE MOON, *MIJA*.
WE MADE A PIZZA TOO! EAT! EAT!
RING RING
RONNIE ANNE, CAN YOU GET THAT?
RING RING
TURN OFF YOUR PHONE ALARM. DO YOU HEAR ME, RONNIE ANNE?

HUH?
RONNIE ANNE! DESPIERTA, IT'S TIME FOR SCHOOL! YOU'LL BE LATE!
OH, MAN, GUESS WE SPENT WAY TOO MUCH TIME WORKING ON THIS MOON PROJECT! LET'S GO!
WOOF!
THANK YOU FOR SUBMITTING YOUR SPACE-THEMED SCULPTURES, CLASS! RONNIE ANNE WINS THIS YEAR'S CONTEST!
MAYBE ONE DAY WE'LL ALL BE ABLE TO FLY TO THE MOON TOGETHER AND EXPLORE!
CLAP CLAP
HA HA!
MY GAS POWER MAKES ME FLY HIGHER THAN YOU, CEEJ!
RÁPIDO, CARLOTA, DID YOU COLLECT ALL THE FLOWERS?
PFFFT
WE'RE NOT SO FAR OFF, MS. GALIANO!
END

"A SUPER HARRRD CHOICE"

"A TIE GAME"

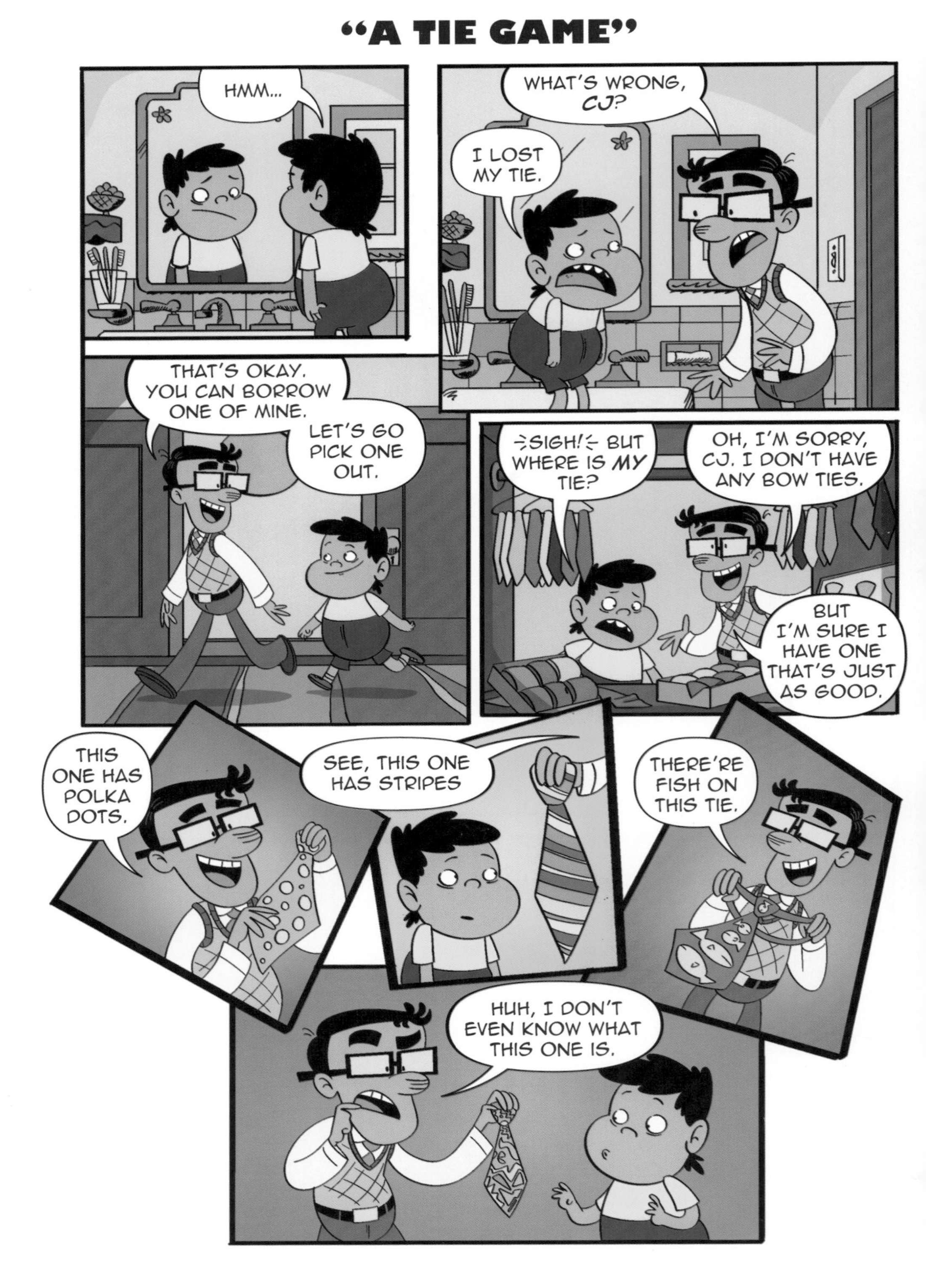
HMM...
WHAT'S WRONG, CJ?
I LOST MY TIE.
THAT'S OKAY. YOU CAN BORROW ONE OF MINE.
LET'S GO PICK ONE OUT.
SIGH! BUT WHERE IS MY TIE?
OH, I'M SORRY, CJ. I DON'T HAVE ANY BOW TIES.
BUT I'M SURE I HAVE ONE THAT'S JUST AS GOOD.
THIS ONE HAS POLKA DOTS.
SEE, THIS ONE HAS STRIPES
THERE'RE FISH ON THIS TIE.
HUH, I DON'T EVEN KNOW WHAT THIS ONE IS.

THIS ONE!
UH, I'M NOT SURE IF YOU REALLY WANT TO WEAR--
DID YOU NEED ME TO HELP TIE THAT FOR--
I GOT IT, DAD!
QUÉ GUAPO, CJ!
YOU LOOK GREAT, MIJO!
BONITO!
IF YOU NEED ANY FASHION TIPS, PAPA, JUST ASK CJ.
MAYBE I SHOULD GO CHANGE TOO?
END

"SERGIO'S BIG BREAK"

EHH, ONE AND TO... NO PAIN, NO STARDOM. GOTTA LOOK FLY!
OKAY, SERGIO, TRY STICKING OUT YOUR NECK A LITTLE FOR YOUR POSING... LIKE THIS!
OH, YEAH, I'M A NATURAL!
NEXT, TAKE OFF YOUR HAIR MASK IN 20 MINUTES AND YOU'LL HAVE GORGEOUS SHINY HAIR FOR THE SHOOT!
THE NEXT DAY...
ALMOST DONE SETTING UP THE PHOTO-SHOOT. ARE YOU READY, SERGIO?
MY WARDROBE CAME JUST IN TIME, GONNA GO CHANGE!
PERFECTO! THIS IS GONNA BE ***SO*** GOOD!
GASP! UH-OH!
MY SUIT IS NOTHING LIKE THE PICTURE, WHAT A RIP-OFF!

WELL, WE GOTTA TAKE THE PICTURES ANYWAY, GIVE IT YOUR BEST SHOT, SERGIO!
YOU'RE RIGHT, NOTHING CAN STOP ME!
FLASH
YIKES!
OH, THIS IS GONNA BE GOOD!
RIP
FLASH
STILL GOT IT!
WHO WANTS TO TRY MY CRUMBLY CHOCOLATE CAKE?
ABUELA, WATCH OUT FOR THE CABLES!
NOOO!
GET IN MY BELLY!
GASP!
OOF! OH, CRACKERS!
PERDÓN, SERGIO!

ALRIGHT, SERGIO, I THINK WE GOT IT!
FLASH
AYY, MY MODELING CAREER IS OVER!
HA! WHEN DID IT START?
WEEKS LATER...
COO COO!
COOO!
SANCHO! WHY ARE YOU ALL TALKING ABOUT ME?
BIRD
HUH? THEY LOVED ME!?
BIRD
GASP! IT WORKED?!
CUTTING EDGE!
INNOVATIVE!
MODERN CLASSIC!
BIRD
I'M STILL A STAR, BABY!
END

"LIMITED EDITION"

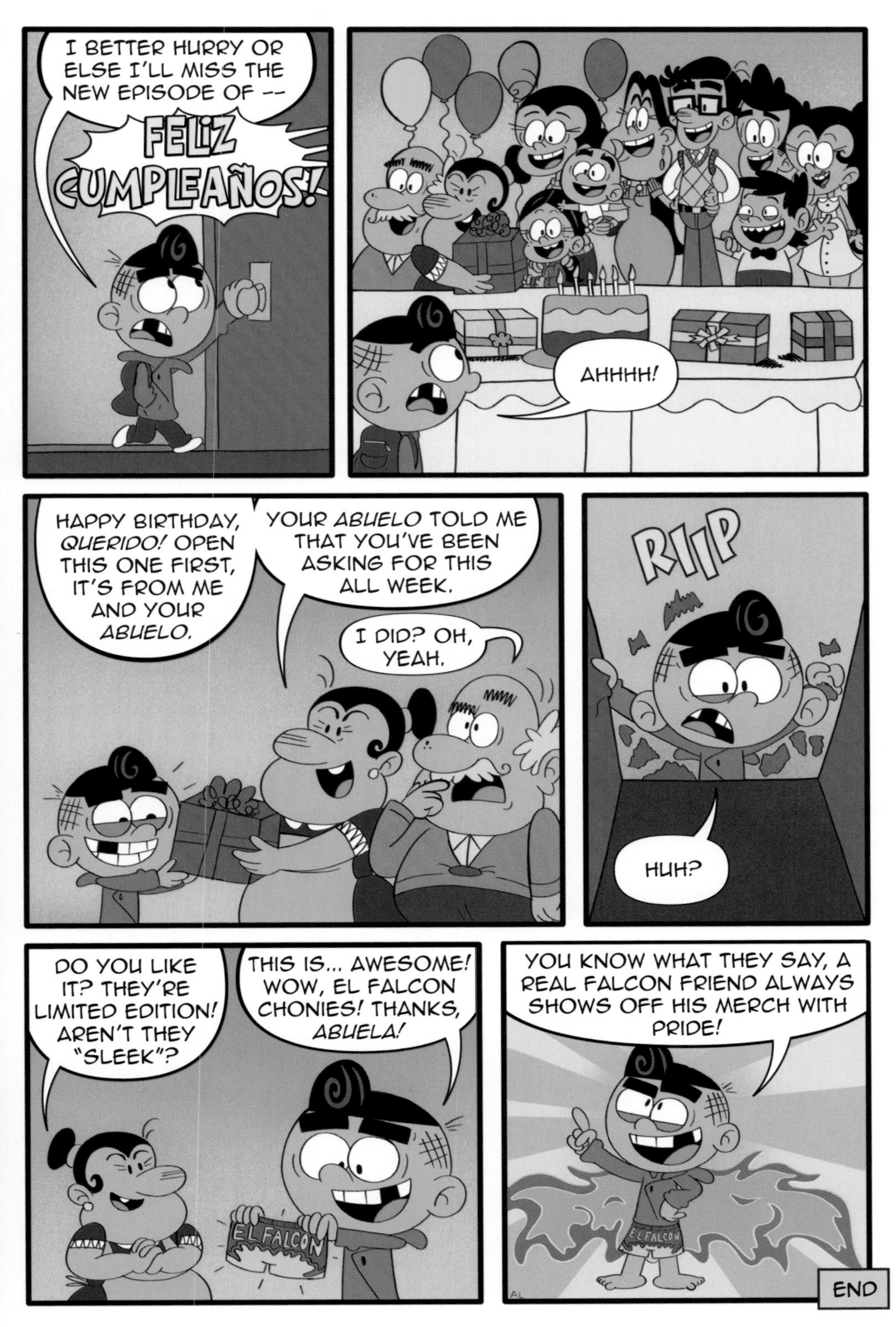

I BETTER HURRY OR ELSE I'LL MISS THE NEW EPISODE OF --
FELIZ CUMPLEAÑOS!
AHHHH!
HAPPY BIRTHDAY, *QUERIDO!* OPEN THIS ONE FIRST, IT'S FROM ME AND YOUR *ABUELO.*
YOUR *ABUELO* TOLD ME THAT YOU'VE BEEN ASKING FOR THIS ALL WEEK.
I DID? OH, YEAH.
RIIP
HUH?
DO YOU LIKE IT? THEY'RE LIMITED EDITION! AREN'T THEY "SLEEK"?
THIS IS... AWESOME! WOW, EL FALCON CHONIES! THANKS, *ABUELA!*
EL FALCON
YOU KNOW WHAT THEY SAY, A REAL FALCON FRIEND ALWAYS SHOWS OFF HIS MERCH WITH PRIDE!
EL FALCON
END

nickelodeon GRAPHIC NOVELS AVAILABLE FROM PAPERCUTZ

THE LOUD HOUSE
#1
"There Will Be Chaos"

THE LOUD HOUSE
#2
"There Will Be More Chaos"

THE LOUD HOUSE
#3
"Live Life Loud!"

THE LOUD HOUSE
#4
"Family Tree"

THE LOUD HOUSE
#5
"After Dark"

THE LOUD HOUSE
#6
"Loud & Proud"

THE LOUD HOUSE
#7
"The Struggle is Real"

THE LOUD HOUSE
#8
"Livin' La Casa Loud!"

THE LOUD HOUSE
#9
"Ultimate Hangout"

THE LOUD HOUSE
#10
"The Many Faces of Lincoln Loud"

THE LOUD HOUSE
#11
"Who's the Loudest?"

THE LOUD HOUSE
#12
"The Case of the Stolen Drawers"

THE LOUD HOUSE
#13
"Lucy Rolls the Dice"

THE LOUD HOUSE
#14
"Guessing Games"

THE LOUD HOUSE
#15
"The Missing Linc"

COMING SOON

THE LOUD HOUSE
#16
"Loud and Clear"

WATCH OUT FOR PAPERCUTZ™

¡Hola! Welcome to the totally-new THE CASAGRANDES #3 "Brand Stinkin' New," from Papercutz, those multi-generational folks dedicated to publishing great graphic novels for all ages. I'm Jim Salicrup, the Editor-in-Chief and despite being "Brand Stinkin' Old," I can still connect with my inner child who sometimes seems a lot like Ronnie Anne's best bud, Lincoln Loud. Anyway, I'm here to make sure that you're aware of the other Nickelodeon graphic novels published by Papercutz, as well as to announce a couple of Papercutz personnel changes (Pretty exciting, eh?).

Of course, if you're a fan of both Papercutz and Nickelodeon–and who isn't?--you already know that Papercutz proudly publishes the on-going hit series, THE LOUD HOUSE, as well as offering up extra-special editions of THE LOUD HOUSE as well. As if that wasn't enough, those wonderful individual volumes of THE LOUD HOUSE graphic novels are also collected in THE LOUD HOUSE 3 IN 1 series, which collects 3 regular volumes of THE LOUD HOUSE in every volume. If you enjoy the adventures of Lincoln Loud, as well as his ten (count 'em!) sisters, Lori, Leni, Luna, Luan, Lynn, Lucy, Lola, Lana, Lisa, and Lily, Papercutz has made sure you have several ways to enjoy them in comics form–the regular series, the specials, and the 3 IN 1s!

For fans of THE CASAGRANDES, this volume is special for a couple of reasons aside from featuring the Casagrandes in lots of enjoyable comic stories. First, being the third graphic novel of THE CASAGRANDES, that makes it possible for there to soon be the first (of many, we hope) THE CASAGRANDES 3 IN 1! (Hmm, maybe we should call it *Tres en Uno*?) After all, we couldn't have published THE CASAGRANDES 3 IN 1 before we published three graphic novels of THE CASAGRANDES, right? This is great news if you're just joining us and were unable to find the first two graphic novels of THE CASAGRANDES.

But don't think we're just trying to sell you something! We always strongly suggest looking for THE CASAGRANDES (and every other Papercutz graphic novel) at your library. And if it's not immediately available at your library, they may be willing to put it on a pull list for you or even order it for you from another library! How great is that?

As for the second special thing about this third graphic novel of THE CASAGRANDES, it actually is all "Brand Stinkin' New"! While our first two volumes included a few stories originally published in THE LOUD HOUSE graphic novels, every story presented in this volume has never been published anywhere else before. And that's going to continue in all THE CASAGRANDES graphic novels yet to come (well, except for the 3 IN 1's, of course!).

Another hit series on Nickelodeon is THE SMURFS, and Papercutz is smurfed to present THE SMURFS in multiple formats as well. THE SMURFS TALES brings you not only the Smurfs in their latest adventures, but other Smurftastic characters from Peyo, the creator of the Smurfs. Characters such as *Johan and Peewit* and *Benny Breakiron*. THE SMURFS 3 IN 1 series collects the earlier individual volumes of THE SMURFS that were published by Papercutz, so you'll have plenty of Smurfs to enjoy!

For those of you who saw the *Watch Out for Papercutz* column in THE CASAGRANDES #2, you may recall we said good-bye (and wished her great success in all her future endeavors) to Joan Hilty, the multi-talented person who was the Nickelodeon Comics Editor ever since Papercutz started publishing Nickelodeon graphic novels. Now we must say good-bye to Papercutz Managing Editor Jeff Whitman, who after seven years at Papercutz, where he co-edited nearly everything with me and was the main editor on THE LOUD HOUSE and THE CASAGRANDES, he has decided to move on... to Nickelodeon!

That's right, Jeff is the new Comics Editor at Nickelodeon and we couldn't be happier for him. Stepping in to take over editing all THE LOUD HOUSE and THE CASAGRANDES graphic novels at Papercutz is erstwhile Papercutz Editorial Intern Karlo Antunes, and our new Assistant Managing Editor is Stephanie Brooks. While Joan Hilty may no longer be involved with our graphic novels, I'm thrilled that Jeff, Karlo, and Stephanie are. Everyone is super-excited and I suspect the very best is yet to come! Don't miss THE CASAGRANDES #4 "Friends and Family"—it's going to be *el mejor*!

Gracias,

Jim

STAY IN TOUCH!

EMAIL:	salicrup@papercutz.com
WEB:	papercutz.com
TWITTER:	@papercutzgn
INSTAGRAM:	@papercutzgn
FACEBOOK:	PAPERCUTZGRAPHICNOVELS
FANMAIL:	Papercutz, 160 Broadway, Suite 700, East Wing, New York, NY 10038

Go to papercutz.com and sign up for the free Papercutz e-newsletter

Exclusive preview of THE LOUD HOUSE BACK TO SCHOOL SPECIAL

"SLEEPLESS IN PRESCHOOL"

THE LOUD HOUSE BACK TO SCHOOL SPECIAL will be on sale soon, don't be tardy!